TWO MOMS, THE ZARK, AND ME

by Johnny Valentine

illustrated by Angelo Lopez

ALYSON
WONDERLAND

an imprint of Alyson Publications, Inc.

To Dan
J.V.

to Andy, Lilia, Peter, and Nancy
A.L.

With special appreciation to Forman Brown, the best editor anyone could have.
—*J.V.*

Text copyright © 1993 by Johnny Valentine. Illustrations copyright © 1993 by Angelo Lopez.
All rights reserved.
Typeset in the United States of America; printed in Hong Kong.

Published in hardcover by Alyson Wonderland,
an imprint of Alyson Publications, Inc., 40 Plympton St., Boston, Mass. 02118.
Distributed in England by GMP Publishers, P.O. Box 247, London N17 9QR, England.

First edition: December 1993

2 4 5 3 1

ISBN 1-55583-236-9

It was raining, that day, when I got out of bed.
The grass was all wet, so I stayed in and read.
Then right after lunch, when the sun lit the sky,
We went off to the park, my two moms and I.

As we walked through the entrance,
We met my moms' friend.
When those three start to talk,
They can talk without end.

A juggler was juggling.
I went over to see.
But very soon he stopped,
And walked away from me.

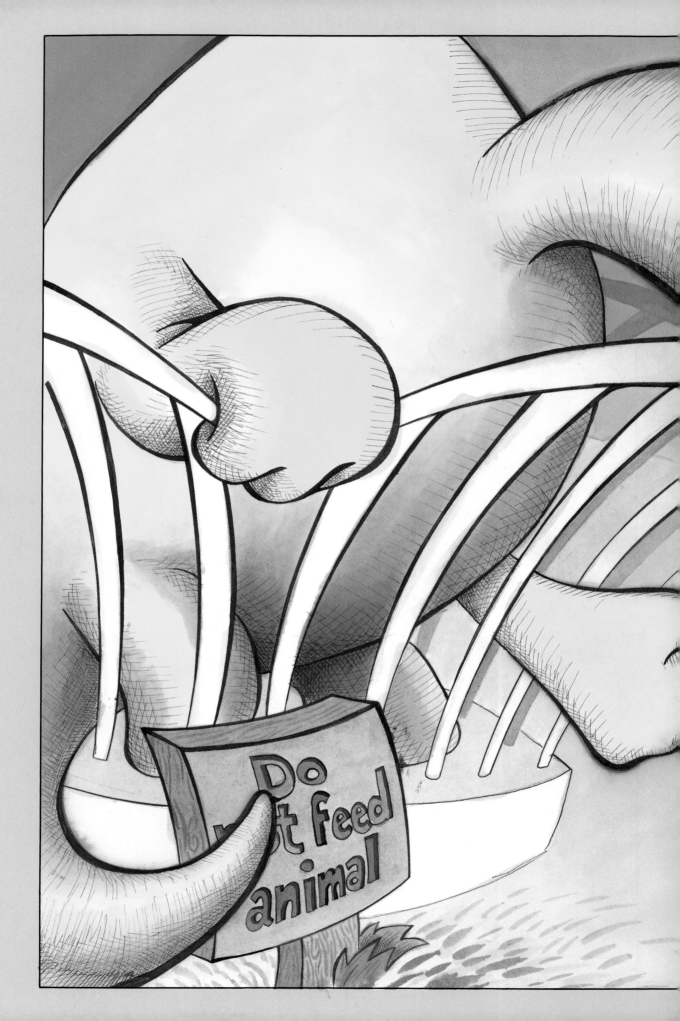

I followed behind
As he walked through the park,
Till we got to the zoo,
Where I saw a tame Zark.
The Zark is so rare,
They once thought it extinct.
But the Zark seemed to like me.
She saw me...

...and winked.

A Zark likes to play,
As I shortly found out,
When I got on her head,
And slid down from her snout...
To her tail — which she flicked —
And I suddenly flew...

So high in the sky, I was scared! You'd be, too!
A whole flock of pigeons was fluttering by.
I thought I could join them! I thought I could fly!

But I found that I couldn't. I tumbled, instead.
If it weren't for that Zark, I'd have lit on my head.

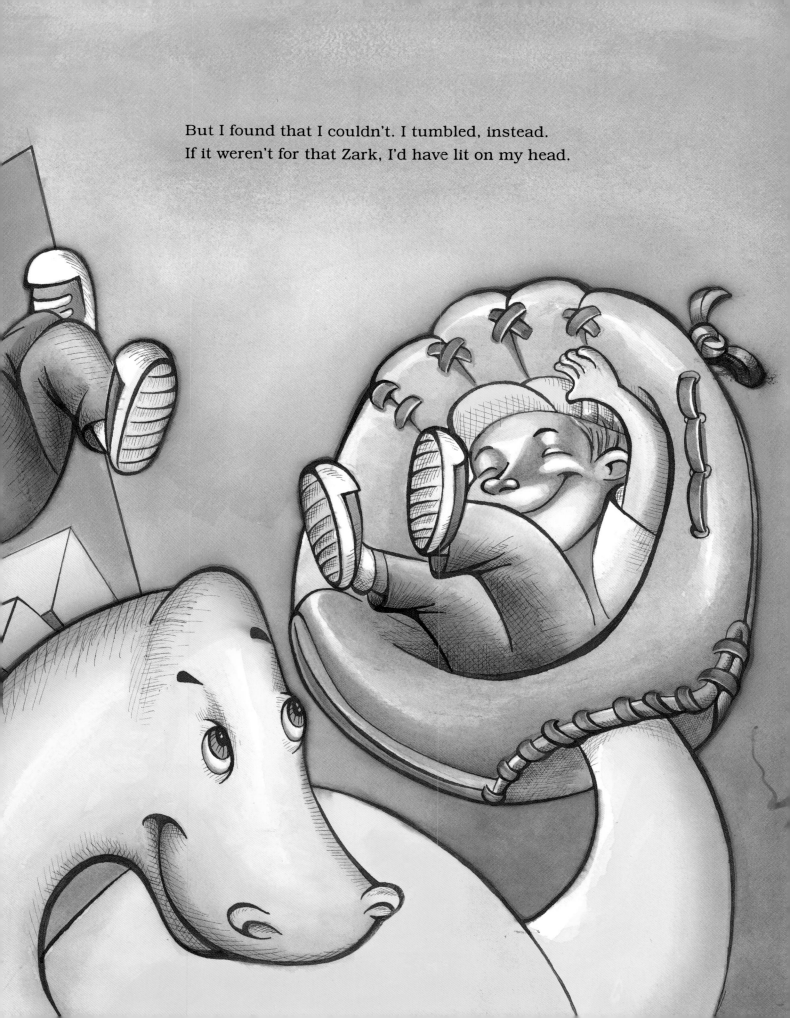

I decided at last I should be on my way,
So I started to walk — then I stopped in dismay.
I stared at the acres of park I had crossed.
Which way were my moms? The fact is, I was...

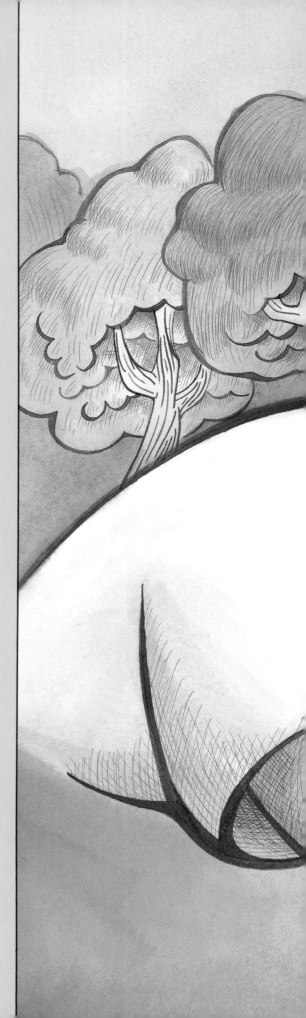

Lost.

I saw skyscrapers, trees, and a distant church steeple,
But my moms weren't in sight, amidst all of those people.

"I'm lost!" I explained, to a couple beside me.
They both looked down slowly,
And carefully eyed me.

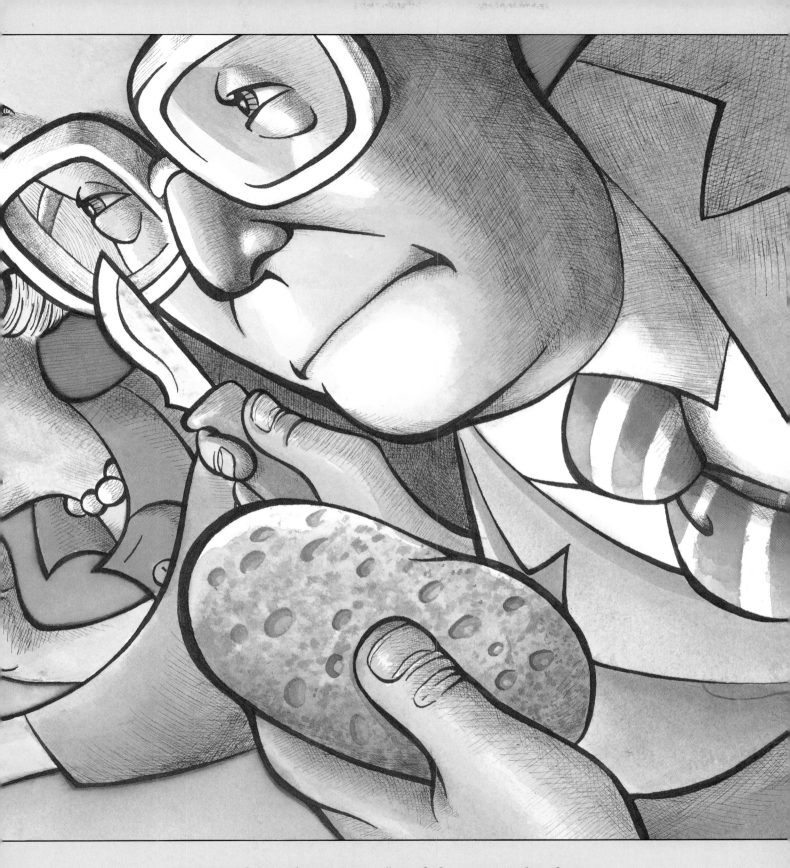

"You just leave things to us," said the man with a frown.
"We are the McFinks, and we're well known in town.
We'll help find your parents. It's really no bother.
But first, please, describe your mother and father."

"Oh, our family," I said, "is unlike some others.
I don't have a dad. But I have two great mothers."

"Two moms? And no dads? I'm shocked!" said McFink.
"It's wrong! It's a sin! Not at all how I think!
The only true family's a family like ours:
With a mom, and a dad, and two kids, and two cars.
And a house, and a yard, and a dog (or a cat).
You just don't have a family if you don't have all that."

I replied, "Though I know this will not seem polite,
From the books I have read, I do not think you're right.
Life is just not that simple," I cautiously said.

And with that, both McFinks turned a little bit red.

"There is no need to read. There is no need to think.
We have done all that FOR you!" roared Mr. McFink.

"You're lucky we found you.
We'll take you away,
And we'll find you a family
That WE deem okay.
Right there," said McFink,
"See those folks with the gnu?
I believe they would make
Perfect parents for you.
They have one child right now,
So they still need another.
Come on, kid, let's meet
Your new father and mother."

And then the McFinks
Seized both of my hands,
And they pulled me along,
As they barked out commands.

"Don't try to escape.
There's not a thing you can do,"
Chortled Mrs. McFink,
"We have GREAT plans for you!"

I would not let them do this!
It simply wasn't right!
So I jerked my hands away,
With all of my might.
They let go. And I ran.
I ran to be free!
I ran because Mr. and Mrs. McFink
Had too many plans for me!

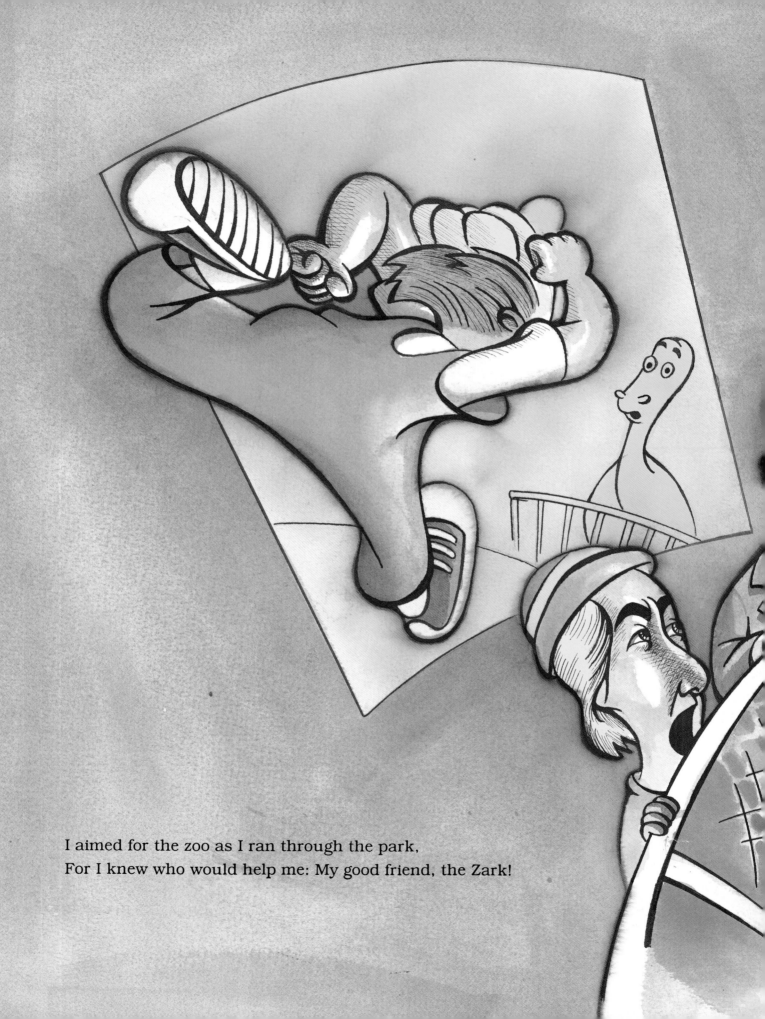

I aimed for the zoo as I ran through the park,
For I knew who would help me: My good friend, the Zark!

"Save me!" I hollered. "It's me, Zark! It's me!
The McFinks want to catch me. I've got to get free!"
The Zark dropped her head and I sat on her crown.
The Zark raised her neck — and I quickly slid down.

The McFinks ran up then, and their rage looked intense.
Yet they couldn't reach me — for between us was the fence.

But my joy did not last, for I watched, with a frown
As the Zark turned against me! She bent her neck down...
...And then Mr. McFink scrambled up on her head.
Now I could not get free ... I'd be captured instead!
"No, Zark, no!" I cried. "You don't know what he intends!
Let me get away, please! I thought that we were friends!"

But the Zark raised her head high, ignoring my plea,
As she sent McFink sliding RIGHT STRAIGHT DOWN AT ME!

Then ... the Zark flicked her tail ... up flew McFink...

And to both our surprises, landed — splash! —
In the drink!

"Now go find your moms," said the Zark with a wink,
"While I look for a towel for Mr. McFink."

I looked all around as I frantically searched,
From the bridge by the pond where the pigeons all perched
To the top of the hill with the merry-go-round.
But no luck. I was lost. My moms weren't to be found.

I walked faster and faster, then started to jog.
Till I found myself standing face-to-face with a dog!

"You look lost!" boomed a voice, from above the dog's head.
I looked up at the owner. "That's quite right," I said.

"I'm MJ," said the voice, "and my friend here is Don.
Let US help you find where your parents have gone."

"No thanks, I have had quite enough help today,"
I replied, as I looked for a fast getaway.

"Now wait," said MJ, "before you go leave us,
 We know we can help. Please do believe us."

"The McFinks said that too," I replied to MJ,
"Then they went and attempted … to give me away!
When they learned that I have two great moms but no dad,
They tried to insist that my family was bad."

"Ah, we know the McFinks,
And they love to condemn
Any family that isn't
Precisely like them,"
Explained Don.
"But one day,
They will get some surprises,
For real families come
In all forms and all sizes.
Our own family, right here,
Includes MJ and me,
Zach, Justin, Francois,
Amelia, and Lee."

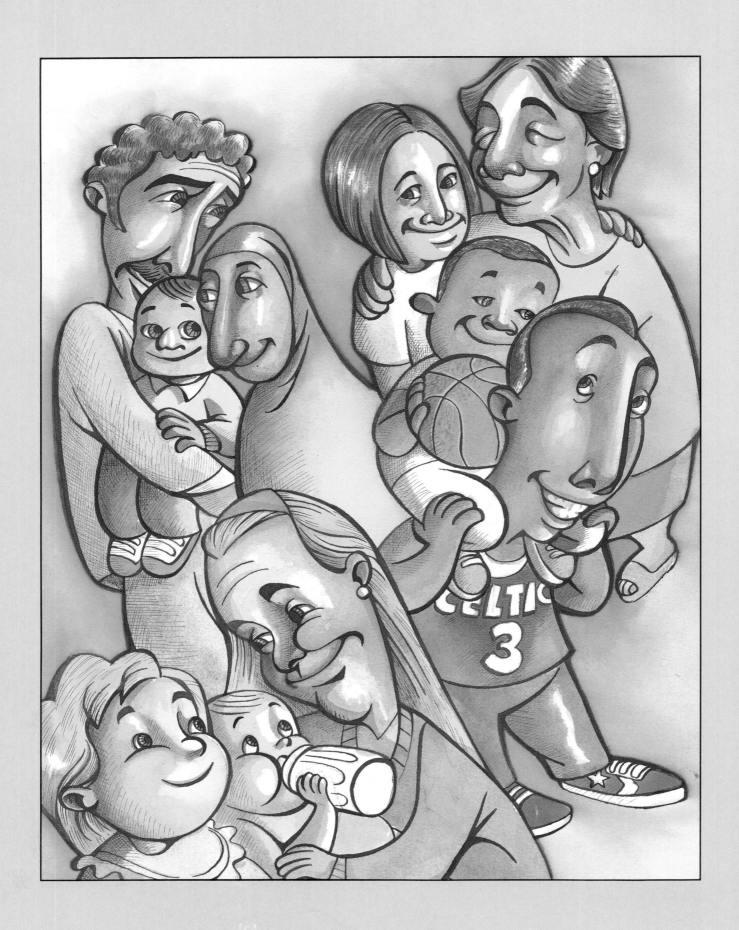

"There are small families, too," Don pointed. "There's one.
That's the Wills, who consist of just father and son.
We wanted more kids, when our family was small;
That's why we went out and adopted them all.
I'd trade families with no one, not even the Wills,"
Don went on, "though I'd love to trade grocery bills!"

"Jenny Lee has one mom and one dad, but in May
She draws TWO cards to celebrate each Mother's Day.
She makes one for her mom, and one for Aunt Sue.
You see, that's her dad's sister, who lives with them too."

"Some things are important. And some things are not.
What matters is this: Your moms love you a lot.
Don't fret about what the McFinks try to tell you.
You don't have to buy what they want to sell you."

"And now," said MJ, "without further ado,
Let's quickly unite your two moms and you."
And somehow, right away, I trusted these two.

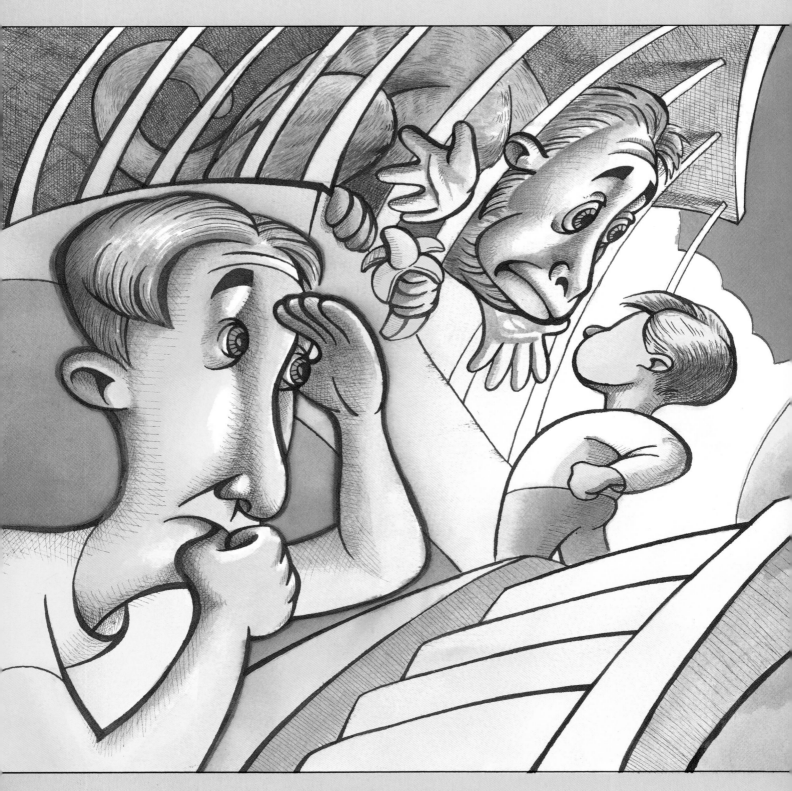

We looked all around in the zoo and the park,
We even went over and asked if the Zark
Would give us a lift. When she smiled and said yes....
I could see miles around — but with still no success.

We looked in the monkey house,
Then with the bears.
We looked behind boulders,
And under the stairs.

"This just isn't working,"
MJ and Don frowned.
Then Don said, "Let's go ask
At the park's Lost and Found.
I'm sure they'll be happy
To give us some help,
As soon as those women—"
                    Then I let out a yelp.
And I hollered and jumped
And shouted with glee.
I yelped, "THOSE are my MOMS!
And they're looking for me!"

My moms gave a big thank-you to Don and MJ,
Then all of us went to the playground to play.

As we got to the swings, the McFinks strutted by.
"We DO not approve!" I could hear them both sigh.

They muttered and sputtered, looking terribly grim,
And when Don laughed a little, they glared back at him.

I felt a bit sorry for those two McFinks
Who are certain they're thinking what everyone thinks,
And I do hope that one of these days they will find
That truly good families aren't all of one kind.

And even McFinks, then, will have to agree,
We're a wonderful family, my two moms and me.